SAN FRANCISCO

49ERS

BY JOSH ANDERSON

Stride

An Imprint of The Child's World®

childsworld.com

The Child's World
childsworld.com

Published by The Child's World®
800-599-READ • www.childsworld.com

Photography Credits
Cover: © Thearon W. Henderson / Stringer / Getty Images; page 1: © Africa Studio / Shutterstock; page 3: © Cliff Hawkins / Staff / Getty Images; page 5: © Christian Petersen / Staff / Getty Images; page 6: © Hulton Archive / Staff / Getty Images; page 9: © Julio Aguilar / Stringer / Getty Images; page 10: © Jason O. Watson / Stringer / Getty Images; page 11: © stevezmina1 / Getty Images; page 12: © Thearon W. Henderson / Stringer / Getty Images; page 12: © Steph Chambers / Staff / Getty Images; page 13: © Ezra Shaw / Staff / Getty Images; page 13: © Ezra Shaw / Staff / Getty Images; page 14: © Jamie Squire / Staff / Getty Images; page 15: © Thearon W. Henderson / Stringer / Getty Images; page 16: © Jed Jacobsohn / Staff / Getty Images; page 16: © Ai Wire-EDWARD LARSON / "Ai Wire Photo Service" / Newscom; page 17: © Otto Greule Jr / Stringer / Getty Images; page 17: © Mike Powell / Staff / Getty Images; page 18: © Al Golub/ZUMA Press / Newscom; page 18: © Jonathan Daniel / Stringer / Getty Images; page 19: © Streeter Lecka / Staff / Getty Images; page 19: © Sean M. Haffey / Staff / Getty Images; page 20: © Ezra Shaw / Staff / Getty Images; page 20: © Christian Petersen / Staff / Getty Images; page 21: © Lachlan Cunningham / Stringer / Getty Images; page 21: © Ezra Shaw / Staff / Getty Images; page 22: © Jonathan Daniel / Stringer / Getty Images; page 23: © SportsChrome / Newscom; page 23: © stevezmina1 / Getty Images; page 25: © Rick Stewart / Stringer / Getty Images; page 26: © Cliff Welch/Icon SMI / Newscom; page 29: © Steve Grayson / Staff / Getty Images

ISBN Information
9781503857919 (Reinforced Library Binding)
9781503860650 (Portable Document Format)
9781503862012 (Online Multi-user eBook)
9781503863378 (Electronic Publication)

LCCN 2021952641

Printed in the United States of America

BRINGING THE WORLD TO YOUNG READERS 1968

TABLE OF CONTENTS

GO 49ERS!

The San Francisco 49ers compete in the National Football **League's** (NFL's) National Football Conference (NFC). They play in the NFC West **division**, along with the Arizona Cardinals, Los Angeles Rams, and Seattle Seahawks. Fans in San Francisco have been lucky! Their 49ers have won the **Super Bowl** five times. Only two NFL teams have won the big game more often. And although they lost both games, the 49ers have been to the Super Bowl twice since 2012. Let's learn more about the 49ers!

NFC WEST DIVISION

Arizona Cardinals

Los Angeles Rams

San Francisco 49ers

Seattle Seahawks

SAN FRANCISCO TIGHT END GEORGE KITTLE CAUGHT FOUR PASSES IN SUPER BOWL 54.

BECOMING THE 49ERS

The San Francisco 49ers began playing in 1946 as part of the All-America Football Conference (AAFC). They joined the NFL in 1949 when the two leagues combined. The team was named after the men and women who traveled west during the 1849 Gold Rush in search of adventure and riches. The 49ers have been one of the NFL's most successful franchises. They have appeared in seven Super Bowls. The team last won the big game after the 1994 season, when they defeated the San Diego Chargers in Super Bowl 29.

QUARTERBACK Y. A. TITTLE PLAYED IN 113 GAMES FOR THE 49ERS FROM 1951 TO 1960.

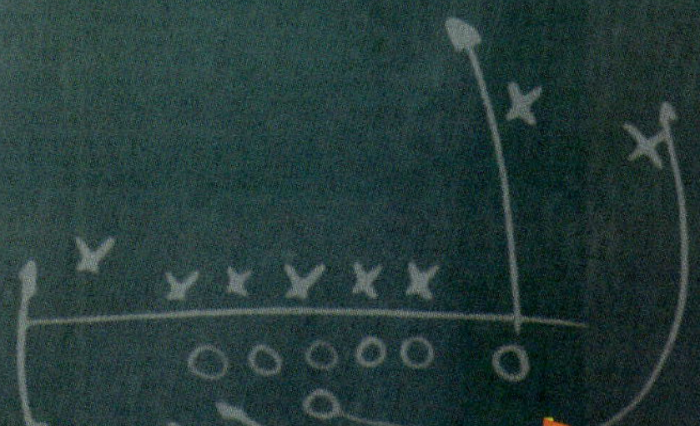

BY THE NUMBERS

The 49ers have won **FIVE** Super Bowls.

21 division titles for the 49ers

505 points scored by the team in 1994—a 49ers record!

15 wins for the 49ers in 1984

THE 49ERS SELECTED WIDE RECEIVER DEEBO SAMUEL (LEFT) WITH A SECOND-ROUND PICK IN THE 2019 NFL DRAFT.

ALTHOUGH THE 49ERS REPRESENT SAN FRANCISCO, THE TEAM'S HOME FIELD IS ACTUALLY LOCATED MUCH CLOSER TO SAN JOSE, CALIFORNIA.

GAME DAY

The 49ers have had three different homes since joining the NFL. From 1946 until 1971, the team played in Kezar **Stadium** in San Francisco's Golden Gate Park. Then, from 1971 until 2013, they shared Candlestick Park with the San Francisco Giants baseball team. Candlestick Park was known for being very cold and windy. In 2014, the 49ers moved to Levi's Stadium, located in Santa Clara, California, about 40 miles (64 km) south of San Francisco. On game days, Levi's Stadium holds about 68,500 fans.

We're Famous!

Legendary 49ers quarterback Joe Montana became famous far beyond the city of San Francisco. He was even made into a cartoon character once! Montana appeared in a season 20 episode of *The Simpsons* called "Double, Double, Boy in Trouble." In a humorous moment, Bart Simpson drives by something that looks like a poster of Joe Montana and says, "Cool poster." Montana pokes his head out of the picture and says, "It's not a poster."

UNIFORM

RED

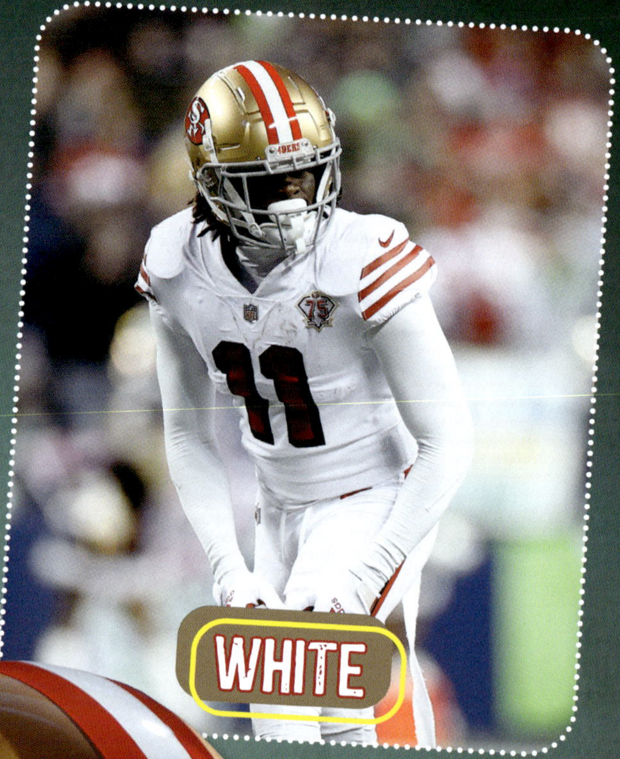

WHITE

Truly Weird

It's fairly common for running backs to catch **touchdown** passes. But it's much less common for wide receivers to rush for touchdowns. Deebo Samuel had other ideas during the 2021 season, though. The wide receiver scored eight rushing touchdowns in 2021. He also had rushing touchdowns in five-straight games. Neither of those accomplishments has happened since before the Super Bowl existed!

Alternate Jersey

Sometimes teams wear an alternate jersey that is different from their home and away jerseys. It might be a bright color or have a unique theme. For a 2017 game against the Los Angeles Rams, the 49ers wore all-black uniforms. Unfortunately, the new look proved unlucky and San Francisco lost the game!

49ERS FANS GET AS LOUD AS THEY CAN BEFORE GAMES, TRYING TO ENERGIZE THE PLAYERS ON THE FIELD.

TEAM SPIRIT

Going to a game at Levi's Stadium can be a ton of fun! Every time the 49ers get a first down, the crowd yells, "Ahoo! Ahoo! Ahoo!" The San Francisco 49ers Gold Rush Cheerleaders entertain fans during breaks in the action and at halftime. They're joined by Sourdough Sam. He's named for sourdough bread, a local food many people associate with San Francisco. Sourdough Sam is a giant costumed character. He is meant to look like the people who came to California during the 1849 California Gold Rush looking for gold.

SOURDOUGH SAM

HEROES OF HISTORY

Frank Gore

Running Back | 2005–2014

In ten seasons with the 49ers, Gore rushed for more than 1,000 yards eight times. His 11,073 yards rushing are the most in team history. He helped lead the team to its appearance in Super Bowl 47. Gore was chosen for five **Pro Bowls** during his time in San Francisco.

Ronnie Lott

Defensive Back | 1981–1990

Lott is San Francisco's all-time leader with 51 interceptions. He led the NFL with ten interceptions in 1986. Lott anchored the defense for four 49ers teams that won the Super Bowl. The ten-time Pro Bowler is a member of the Pro Football **Hall of Fame**. He was also selected for the NFL's 100th Anniversary All-Time Team.

Joe Montana

Quarterback | 1979–1992

Montana led the 49ers to four Super Bowl victories during his career, along with a 100–39 record in the regular season. He was selected as the NFL's **Most Valuable Player** (MVP) after the 1989 and 1990 seasons. Montana was picked for eight Pro Bowls. He was inducted into the Pro Football Hall of Fame in 2000.

Steve Young

Quarterback | 1987–1999

Young won the NFL's MVP Award twice. He led the 49ers to a 91–33 regular season record as their starting quarterback. Young also led San Francisco to victory in Super Bowl 29. He led the league in passing touchdowns four times. The seven-time Pro Bowler is a member of the Pro Football Hall of Fame.

The 49ers defeat the Cincinnati Bengals 26–21 in Super Bowl 16.

In Super Bowl 29, San Francisco defeats the San Diego Chargers 49–26.

BIG DAYS

JANUARY 20, 2013

With a trip to Super Bowl 47 on the line, the 49ers defeat the Atlanta Falcons 28–24 in the NFC Championship Game.

JANUARY 19, 2020

The 49ers advance to Super Bowl 54 with a 37–20 win over the Green Bay Packers in the NFC Championship Game.

MODERN-DAY MARVELS

Nick Bosa

Defensive End | Debut: 2019

Bosa finished his **rookie** season with nine **sacks** in 2019. He was chosen as the NFL's Defensive Rookie of the Year. After missing most of 2020 with an injury, Bosa came back strong in 2021. He finished with 15.5 sacks and tied for first in the NFL with 21 tackles for a loss.

George Kittle

Tight End | Debut: 2017

Kittle excels as both a blocking tight end and receiver. He's finished with more than 1,000 yards receiving twice in his career. Since entering the NFL, Kittle has the second-most receiving yards of any player at the tight end position. He's been selected for the Pro Bowl three times.

Deebo Samuel

Wide Receiver | Debut: 2019

Samuel had his first season with more than 1,000 receiving yards in 2021, when he finished with 1,405 yards. His average of 18.2 yards per reception led the NFL in 2021. Samuel also set the modern-era record for rushing touchdowns by a wide receiver in a season. He rushed for eight touchdowns in 2021.

Fred Warner

Linebacker | Debut: 2018

In 2018, Warner became the first NFL rookie since 2000 to start his career with four-straight games with at least ten tackles. Warner has led the 49ers in tackles in each of the four years he's played in the NFL. He was picked for his first Pro Bowl in 2020.

JERRY RICE'S FINAL GAME AS A 49ER CAME AT THE END OF THE 2000 NFL SEASON. HE CAUGHT SIX PASSES FOR 61 YARDS IN A LOSS TO THE DENVER BRONCOS.

THE GOAT

GREATEST OF ALL TIME

JERRY RICE

In 2010, Rice was chosen by the NFL as its top player of all time. He ranks first all-time in receiving yards with 22,895. His 197 touchdown catches also rank first all-time. Rice led the 49ers to three Super Bowl victories during his career. He was chosen for the Pro Bowl 13 times. He was inducted into the Pro Football Hall of Fame in 2010.

FAN FAVORITE

John Brodie–Quarterback

1957–1973

Brodie endeared himself to fans over 17 seasons with the team, most spent as the 49ers' starting quarterback. He led the league in passing yards three times and passing touchdowns twice. In 1970, he was chosen as the NFL's MVP. Brodie was selected for the Pro Bowl twice during his career.

THE BIG GAME

JANUARY 28, 1990 – SUPER BOWL 24

The 49ers finished with an NFL-best 14–2 record during the 1989 regular season. They fought through the **playoffs** and earned the right to play the Denver Broncos in Super Bowl 24. The Broncos finished the season with an 11–5 record, which was the best in the AFC. In the game's opening minutes, quarterback Joe Montana found wide receiver Jerry Rice for a touchdown pass. It would be Montana's first of five passing touchdowns of the day. Rice finished with 148 yards receiving and three touchdown catches. The 49ers won the game 55–10. It's the largest margin of victory ever in a Super Bowl.

DURING THE 1989 NFL REGULAR SEASON, THE DENVER BRONCOS DEFENSE ALLOWED THE FEWEST POINTS TO OPPOSING TEAMS. THE 49ERS MANAGED TO SCORE 55 POINTS ON THEM IN SUPER BOWL 24.

BILL WALSH LED THE 49ERS TO 92 REGULAR SEASON VICTORIES AND THREE SUPER BOWL TITLES FROM 1979 TO 1988.

AMAZING FEATS

4,278 Passing Yards

In 2000 by
QUARTERBACK
Jeff Garcia

1,695 Rushing Yards

In 2006 by
RUNNING BACK
Frank Gore

1,848 Receiving Yards

In 1995 by
WIDE RECEIVER
Jerry Rice

19.5 Sacks

In 2012 by
DEFENSIVE END
Aldon Smith

ALL-TIME BEST

PASSING YARDS

Joe Montana
35,124

John Brodie
31,548

Steve Young
29,907

RUSHING YARDS

Frank Gore
11,073

Joe Perry
8,689

Roger Craig
7,064

RECEIVING YARDS

Jerry Rice
19,247

Terrell Owens
8,572

Dwight Clark
6,750

SACKS*

Cedrick Hardman
108

Bryant Young
89.5

Tommy Hart
72.5

SCORING

Jerry Rice
1,130

Ray Wersching
979

Tommy Davis
738

INTERCEPTIONS

Ronnie Lott
51

Jimmy Johnson
47

Kermit Alexander
36

*unofficial before 1982

TERRELL OWENS LED THE NFL IN RECEIVING TOUCHDOWNS TWICE DURING HIS TIME AS A 49ER.

GLOSSARY

division (dih-VIZSH-un): a group of teams within the NFL that play each other more frequently and compete for the best record

Hall of Fame (HAHL of FAYM): a museum in Canton, Ohio, that honors the best players in NFL history

league (LEEG): an organization of sports teams that compete against each other

Most Valuable Player (MOHST VAL-yuh-bul PLAY-uhr): a yearly award given to the top player in the NFL

playoffs (PLAY-ahfs): a series of games after the regular season that decides which two teams play in the Super Bowl

Pro Bowl (PRO BOWL): the NFL's All-Star game where the best players in the league compete

rookie (RUH-kee): a player playing in his first season

sack (SAK): when a quarterback is tackled behind the line of scrimmage before he can throw the ball

stadium (STAY-dee-um): a building with a field and seats for fans where teams play

Super Bowl (SOO-puhr BOWL): the championship game of the NFL, played between the winners of the AFC and the NFC

touchdown (TUTCH-down): a play in which the ball is brought into the other team's end zone, resulting in six points

FIND OUT MORE

IN THE LIBRARY

Bulgar, Beth and Mark Bechtel. *My First Book of Football.* New York, NY: Time Inc. Books, 2015.

Carr, Aaron. *San Francisco 49ers*. New York, NY: AV2, 2020.

Jacobs, Greg. *The Everything Kids' Football Book, 7th Edition*. Avon, MA: Adams Media, 2021.

Sports Illustrated Kids. *The Greatest Football Teams of All Time*. New York, NY: Time Inc. Books, 2018.

ON THE WEB

Visit our website for links about the San Francisco 49ers:
childsworld.com/links

Note to parents, teachers, and librarians: We routinely verify our web links to make sure they are safe and active sites. Encourage your readers to check them out!

INDEX

ABOUT THE AUTHOR

Josh Anderson has published over 50 books for children and young adults. His two boys are the greatest joys in his life. Hobbies include coaching his sons in youth basketball, no-holds-barred games of Apples to Apples, and taking long family walks. His favorite NFL team is a secret he'll never share!